Mr Darcy
the Dancing Duck

Written by Alex Field   Illustrated by Peter Carnavas

First published in the UK in 2017
by New Frontier Publishing (Europe) Pty. Ltd.
93 Harbord Street, London SW6 6PN
www.newfrontierpublishing.co.uk

ISBN: 978-1-912076-57-4

A CIP catalogue record for this book is available from the British Library.

Printed in China
10 9 8 7 6 5 4 3 2 1

For my dancing girls, Jessica, Helena and Grace.
AF

For Donna, a Mr Darcy devotee.
PC

Mr Darcy set out for his morning walk.
The sun was shining and the daffodils were beginning to flower.
Spring was in the air.

'Oh dear,' he thought, 'it's dancing season again.'

He said good day to Maria, the mouse, as
she skipped along the path.

He tipped his hat at Bingley, the horse,
who trotted around the field

and smiled at Caroline, the cow, who waltzed out in the pasture.

As he glanced across Pemberley Park, Mr Darcy saw Lizzy
and her sisters dancing around a maypole.
He shook his head and hurried along.

Lizzy ran up to Mr Darcy and asked if he would like to dance.

After all, he was the best looking duck in the district.

'No, thank you,' he replied politely.

Mr Darcy went away feeling sad.

As he walked home, he did not say good day to Maria or tip his hat
at Bingley or even smile at Caroline.

His friends knew something was wrong.
They followed Mr Darcy home.

With a furrowed brow, Mr Darcy waddled around his garden.
Mr Darcy enjoyed waddling: but dancing?

He turned round and round in circles, trying his best to dance.

He ended up on his bottom.

As Caroline and Bingley watched,
Maria gave Mr Darcy a helping hand.

One-two, one-two, round in a circle they went.
First they walked. Then they skipped.

Mr Darcy was a little clumsy at first,

but he soon learned the steps.

Maria thought perhaps it was time for the maypole.
Bingley planted a branch in the ground and Caroline
offered her purple bow. Mr Darcy's bow tie became
the perfect ribbon.

With the help of Bingley and Caroline, music filled the air.

They all agreed that Mr Darcy really looked rather
splendid as he danced around the field.
'I think he's got it,' said Maria, rather proudly.

The next day Mr Darcy went for his morning walk, and
who do you think he saw?

It was Lizzy and her sisters.

Mr Darcy went bright red, but this time ...

he agreed to dance around the maypole with Lizzy.

Round and round they went, with
Maria, Bingley and Caroline looking on.

Mr Darcy couldn't have been happier,
dancing with Lizzy in Pemberley Park.